Hello, Family Members,

Learning to read is one of the most important accomplishments of early childhood. **Hello Reader!** books are designed to help children become skilled readers who like to read. Beginning readers learn to read by remembering frequently used words like "the," "is," and "and"; by using phonics skills to decode new words; and by interpreting picture and text clues. These books provide both the stories children enjoy and the structure they need to read fluently and independently. Here are suggestions for helping your child *before*, *during*, and *after* reading:

Before

• Look at the cover and pictures and have your child predict what the story is about.
• Read the story to your child.
• Encourage your child to chime in with familiar words and phrases.
• Echo read with your child by reading a line first and having your child read it after you do.

During

• Have your child think about a word he or she does not recognize right away. Provide hints such as "Let's see if we know the sounds" and "Have we read other words like this one?"
• Encourage your child to use phonics skills to sound out new words.
• Provide the word for your child when more assistance is needed so that he or she does not struggle and the experience of reading with you is a positive one.
• Encourage your child to have fun by reading with a lot of expression . . . like an actor!

After

• Have your child keep lists of interesting and favorite words.
• Encourage your child to read the books over and over again. Have him or her read to brothers, sisters, grandparents, and even teddy bears. Repeated readings develop confidence in young readers.
• Talk about the stories. Ask and answer questions. Share ideas about the funniest and most interesting characters and events in the stories.

I do hope that you and your child enjoy this book.

—Francie Alexander
Reading Specialist,
Scholastic's Learning Ventures

To Louise,
a friend for all seasons
—M.F.

To Sophia and Jack
—M.S.

Go to www.scholastic.com for web site information on
Scholastic authors and illustrators.

ISBN 0-439-20061-X

Library of Congress Cataloging-in-Publication Data

Fleming, Maria.
    Autumn leaves are falling / by Maria Fleming; illustrated by Melissa Sweet.
        p.   cm.— (Hello reader! Level 1)
    "Cartwheel Books."
    Summary: Children delight in jumping, leaping, crunching, stomping, and raking as
leaves fall down on them.
    ISBN 0-439-20061-X (pbk.)
    [1. Leaves—Fiction. 2. Autumn—Fiction. 3. Stories in rhyme.]
I. Sweet, Melissa, ill.   II. Title.   III. Series.
PZ8.3.F6385   Au 2000
[E]—dc21   99-462280

10 9 8 7 6 5 4 3   00 01 02 03 04
                    Printed in the U.S.A.   23
                    First printing, September 2000

Autumn Leaves Are Falling

by Maria Fleming

Illustrated by
Melissa Sweet

Hello Reader! — Level 1

SCHOLASTIC INC.

New York   Toronto   London   Auckland   Sydney
Mexico City   New Delhi   Hong Kong

Leaves are falling
down, down, down.

Leaves are falling on the town.

Leaves are falling on my hat.

Leaves are falling on my cat.

Leaves are piling up, up, up.

Leaves are covering up my pup.

Leaves are covering up my feet.

Leaves are covering up my street.

We are jumping.

We are leaping.

We are hiding.

We are creeping.

We are crunching.

We are stomping.

We are rolling.

We are romping.

Okay, okay. We've had our fun.
Now grab a rake, everyone.

We rake, rake, rake,
and in a while,

the leaves are all in one big pile!

Oh, let's jump one last time,
and then

we'll rake up
all the leaves again.

Autumn leaves have gone away.

09/06

But they'll be back another day!